THIS WALKER BOOK BELONGS TO:

For

Michael Philip J.C.

_____

For Amelia   S.L.

First published 1995 by Walker Books Ltd
87 Vauxhall Walk, London SE11 5HJ

This edition published 1996

20 19 18 17 16 15 14

Text © 1995 June Crebbin
Illustrations © 1995 Stephen Lambert

The right of June Crebbin and Stephen
Lambert to be identified as author and
illustrator respectively of this work has been
asserted by them in accordance with the
Copyright, Designs and Patents Act 1988

This book has been typeset in Rockwell

Printed in China

All rights reserved

British Library Cataloguing in Publication
Data: a catalogue record for this book is
available from the British Library

ISBN-13: 978-0-7445-4701-6
ISBN-10: 0-7445-4701-6

www.walkerbooks.co.uk

The Train Ride

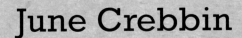

June Crebbin

WALKER BOOKS
AND SUBSIDIARIES
LONDON · BOSTON · SYDNEY · AUCKLAND

Illustrated by
Stephen Lambert

We're off on a journey   Out of the town –

What shall I see?

What shall I see?

Sheep running off
And cows lying down,

That's what I see,
That's what I see.

Over the meadow,
Up on the hill,

What shall I see?
What shall I see?

A mare and her foal
Standing perfectly still,

That's what I see,
That's what I see.

There is a farm
Down a bumpety road –

What shall I see?
What shall I see?

A shiny red tractor
Pulling its load,

That's what I see,
That's what I see.

Here in my seat,
My lunch on my knee,

What shall I see?
What shall I see?

A ticket collector
Smiling at me,

That's what I see,
That's what I see.

Into the tunnel,
Scary and black –

What shall I see?
What shall I see?

My face in a mirror,
Staring back,

That's what I see,
That's what I see.

After the tunnel –
When we come out –

What shall I see?
What shall I see?

A gaggle of geese
Strutting about,

That's what I see,
That's what I see.

Over the treetops,
High in the sky,

What shall I see?
What shall I see?

A giant balloon
Sailing by,

That's what I see,
That's what I see.

Listen! The engine
Is slowing down –

What shall I see?
What shall I see?

A market square,
A seaside town,

That's what I see,
That's what I see.

There is the lighthouse,   The sand and the sea...

Here is the station –

Who shall I see?

There is my grandma

Welcoming me...

Welcoming

me.

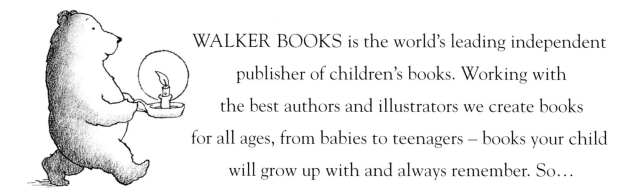

WALKER BOOKS is the world's leading independent publisher of children's books. Working with the best authors and illustrators we create books for all ages, from babies to teenagers – books your child will grow up with and always remember. So…

FOR THE BEST CHILDREN'S BOOKS, LOOK FOR THE BEAR